HAVE YOU READ?

A FOREVER HOME FOR TILLY

LOOK OUT FOR:

A FOREVER HOME FOR LUNA

A FOREVER HOME FOR FLUFFY

A FOREVER HOME FOR PIP

LINDA CHAPMAN

Illustrated By
Sophy Williams

nosy
crow

First published in the UK in 2020 by Nosy Crow Ltd
The Crow's Nest, 14 Baden Place
Crosby Row, London SE1 1YW

www.nosycrow.com

ISBN: 978 1 78800 820 4

Nosy Crow and associated logos are trademarks and/or
registered trademarks of Nosy Crow Ltd.

Text copyright © Linda Chapman and Julie Sykes, 2020
Illustrations © Sophy Williams, 2020

A CIP catalogue record for this book will be available from the British Library.

Printed and bound in Great Britain by Clays Ltd, Elcograf S.p.A.

Papers used by Nosy Crow are made from
wood grown in sustainable forests.

1 3 5 7 9 10 8 6 4 2

For Lara, who is sassy, smart
and full of doggy heart.

CHAPTER 1

"Jack! Look at that cute Border collie puppy!" said Grace.

It was a sunny Friday afternoon and Grace and her twin brother were walking Tiny, their family's enormous dog, in the park. The very fluffy black-and-white

    1

puppy raced towards them, yapping excitedly. Tiny flopped to the ground, his tail wagging, as the puppy pounced at him.

Jack looked around the park. "Who's he with? The only person I can see is Mum."

Their mother was following some way behind with the four dogs she was looking after that day. She ran a doggy day care business called Top Dog.

"Oh! He must have run into the park from the street," said Grace.

A squirrel scampered up a nearby tree trunk. The puppy ran towards it eagerly and tried to climb the tree, its paws scrabbling against the bark.

"He's very lively," said Jack.

"We've got to catch him!" Grace said. "He might run off and get hurt. Take Tiny,

Jack." She handed the lead over and walked towards the puppy. "Come here, pup," she coaxed.

The puppy watched her approaching, then sprang up and raced behind the tree.

"No!" shouted Grace, running after it.

"Wait!" called Jack. "If you chase it, it might get scared and run further. Slow down and stay calm."

Grace sighed. Jack was always telling her to slow down, but she knew her brother was right. She crouched down and called gently, "Here, puppy!"

To her relief, the puppy stopped running. Its ears relaxed and it came towards her. Grace slowly held out her hand, keeping

her fist closed and her palm down, like she knew she was supposed to. The little puppy sniffed her fingers, then huffed and licked her hand all over, its tail wagging. Seeing that it was now happy with her, she stroked its soft back and the puppy jumped into her arms.

"You are so friendly!" she exclaimed. The puppy wriggled, trying to chew the ends of her brown hair.

"Has it got a tag on?" Jack asked.

Grace read the bone-shaped identity tag fastened to the puppy's blue collar. "Yes. His name's Pip. Hello, Pip," she said to the bundle in her arms, feeling her heart melt as she looked into his cheeky dark eyes. Pip had a black face with a narrow white blaze and a cute button nose. The tip of his

tail and his paws were white, as if they'd
been dipped in paint. One of his ears was
pricked but the other wouldn't stand up
and kept flopping over.

"Is there a phone number?" said Jack.
"Should we ask Mum to call it and—"

"I don't think we need to," interrupted
Grace as a young couple ran into the park,
calling out Pip's name. "I think his owners
have just found us!"

"Pip!" exclaimed the woman, spotting
the puppy in Grace's arms. "I'm Jess, his
owner. Oh, you naughty boy!" she said
to the puppy, sounding more worried
than cross. The man joined her as Grace
handed him over.

"We thought we'd lost you," he said,
ruffling the puppy's ears.

"Thanks for catching him," said Jess gratefully. "He's such a nightmare. He keeps going off after other dogs, doesn't he, Alex?"

"And birds, squirrels and people," the man, Alex, added dryly. "We've had him for almost a month and we thought he would have calmed down by now, but if anything, he's getting worse."

"We live in a flat," explained Jess. "We walk him three times a day but it's never enough. He sleeps for a bit and then he's up again, tearing around the place, barking like crazy until we take him out."

"His barking is upsetting our neighbours," said Alex. "He's so friendly, but I'm just not sure we should have got a puppy like him. His parents were both

working sheepdogs and he's got so much energy."

Grace and Jack exchanged a look. It was a twin thing – they often knew exactly what the other was thinking. Jack gave Grace a nod and she turned to the couple.

"It does sound like he might not be the right dog for you. What do you think you will you do?" she asked politely. "Will you keep him or will you try and find him a new home?" She crossed her fingers. It would be wonderful to have a new animal to rehome!

Jess and Alex looked at each other. "I think a new home would be best," said Jess with a sigh. She kissed the wriggling puppy. "I love him to bits but he would be much happier somewhere he can run

around outside all the time. We've also
just found out that I'm going to have a
baby later in the year. I really don't know
how we'll cope with a baby and a dog like
Pip."

"But we don't like the thought of taking
him to a dog shelter," said Alex. "He loves
his cuddles too much."

Excitement rushed through Grace.
"We might be able to help you," she said
eagerly. "Jack and I run Forever Homes."

"We're experts at finding cats and dogs
their forever home," added Jack. "We
always make sure we find them the perfect
owner, and until we do, they live with
us, so they don't feel lonely. Our mum's
over there if you want to talk to her." He
pointed to where Mum was letting the

dogs sniff a lamppost. "She runs Top Dog."

"Oh, that's the lady with the van that looks like a dog?" said Jess. "It always makes me smile when I see it around town."

"Maybe we could have a word with her?" said Alex.

"Sure," said Grace. Although she and Jack were completely in charge of the rehoming business, they were used to people wanting to talk to their mum before handing over their animals. "Mum!" she called, beckoning her.

Mum came over. "Hello," she said, smiling at Alex and Jess. "I'm Sarah Taylor. What a gorgeous puppy," she said as Jess put Pip down so he could say hello to the other dogs. Jess explained the situation.

"Jack and Grace are very good at rehoming animals," said Mum. "And it does sound like it might be the best thing, the kindest thing, if you don't feel you can give him what he needs."

Jess picked Pip up and gave him a big cuddle. "Don't you think that I'm not going to miss you because I will, Pip," she said, her voice sounding squeaky. "But I want you to be happy, that's all that matters." Blinking back a few tears, she swallowed and handed him to Grace. "You should take him now. I don't think I could bear to say goodbye again. We'll come over to sort the paperwork later."

"We promise we'll find him the perfect home," said Jack.

"And we'll look after him really well until we do," added Grace.

The twins watched as Alex put his arm round Jess and they walked away.

"That was a very hard decision for them to make," said Mum. "But they're doing

the right thing. It would be difficult for them to cope with a baby as well, and a flat really isn't a suitable home for a lively Border collie puppy."

"You're a working dog – a sheepdog," Grace told Pip. "We'll find you a new home with lots of space outside."

"And experienced owners who'll train you," Jack added.

Pip yapped happily as if he agreed.

CHAPTER 2

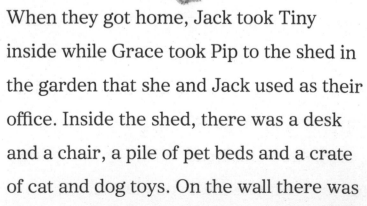

When they got home, Jack took Tiny
inside while Grace took Pip to the shed in
the garden that she and Jack used as their
office. Inside the shed, there was a desk
and a chair, a pile of pet beds and a crate
of cat and dog toys. On the wall there was

a cork board full of photos of all the pets
she and Jack had successfully rehomed.
Grace's heart swelled with pride as she
looked at it. There was nothing that made
her happier than finding an animal their
forever home!

"It'll be your turn next," Grace told Pip,
replacing his identity tag with a Forever
Homes one before unclipping his lead.
The twins kept a pot of metal identity tags
that they used on any animals they were
looking after.

Pip trotted around the office, his bottom
wiggling as he investigated every corner.
When the door opened and Jack came in,
Pip pounced on Jack's feet and barked.

Jack shook his head. "No, I'm not going
to play with you until you calm down."

"I don't think he wants to play," said Grace, watching Pip carefully. He pranced around Jack, nudging his legs with his nose. Grace giggled. "I think he's trying to herd you towards me."

Jack grinned. "You're right. It's the sheepdog in him! You clever little puppy." He picked him up. Pip licked his ear, his little tail going crazy.

"Right, time for you to take a personality test," said Jack, putting Pip down and sitting at the desk. Opening a large blue notebook, he neatly wrote the date and Pip's name.

The Forever Homes personality test helped the twins to find out what an animal was really like so that they could pair them with a suitable person. It gave

them an idea how playful the pet was, how bold and how trainable.

"We already know quite a bit about Pip's personality," said Grace. "He's very friendly, both with people and with other dogs. He's also energetic, lively and inquisitive, and he seems to like herding things."

Jack made some notes. "He doesn't seem to be trained. Let's see if he knows the basic commands." He looked at the puppy, who was sniffing at the crate of toys and called, "Pip, come!"

Pip looked round and wagged his tail.

"Pip, come!" said Grace.

"Grace, don't!" said Jack quickly. "You'll confuse him if we both call him."

Grace sighed. She knew her brother was right. "Sorry," she said, poking her tongue out at him when he turned away.

"Pip, come here!" Jack tried again. Pip ran over to Jack. "Good boy!" Jack made a fuss of him and then took a treat out of a tin on the desk. He held it up. "Now sit."

Pip sat at once. Jack gave him the treat.

"Down," said Jack, pointing at the floor.

As Pip began to lie down, a bird

started to sing outside. The little puppy sprang up and raced to the door, barking.

"No, Pip!" said Jack, picking the puppy up. "You seem to have had some training, but you get distracted very easily."

"I bet he likes to play," said Grace. She picked out some toys from the crate and they took Pip into the garden. They soon found out he absolutely loved games! He played tug with a rope and chased a ball all over the lawn. No matter how many times they threw it, Pip was there, racing after it then dropping it back at their feet so they could throw it again.

"You're definitely going to need a very active owner," said Jack.

"And someone who doesn't have close neighbours," added Grace, as Pip yapped loudly, asking for the ball to be thrown again. "I'll make some posters to put up in the local shops. There has to be someone who's right for him."

Jack nodded. "His perfect home is out there. We just need to find it!"

CHAPTER 3

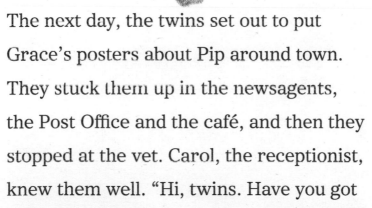

The next day, the twins set out to put
Grace's posters about Pip around town.
They stuck them up in the newsagents,
the Post Office and the café, and then they
stopped at the vet. Carol, the receptionist,
knew them well. "Hi, twins. Have you got

a new animal in for rehoming then?" she asked, seeing the posters in Jack's hand.

"Yes, a Border collie puppy. Please could we put a poster up?" Jack asked.

"Of course. Go ahead," said Carol.

A slim blonde woman in wellies who looked about their mum's age was sitting next to the noticeboard. An old black Labrador with a grey muzzle was lying beside her. He thumped his tail on the floor and lifted his head stiffly as the twins stopped nearby.

"Is it OK if I stroke him?" Grace asked the lady as Jack pinned the poster on the board.

"Oh, yes. He's not infectious, he's just here to see the vet because his arthritis is playing up," said the lady. "He's called Winston."

Grace bent down and stroked him, rubbing behind his ears. He panted happily.

"I like your poster," said the lady, looking at the photo of Pip that Grace had printed off and decorated with a border of bones. Underneath it, Jack had neatly written some information about him and the type of home he was looking for. "It makes mine look very old and shabby." She nodded to the noticeboard, where a tatty poster advertised Apple Tree Farm.

"Oh, do you live there?" said Grace. "We're going on a school trip to Apple Tree Farm this Monday."

"Ah, so you must go to Greenfield's Primary School?" said the lady. "I remember taking the booking. Well, it'll be lovely to see you all. We haven't had a school visit for a while. I really should make some new posters to try and get some more visitors. We need people coming to the farm to help pay for the upkeep of the animals. I wonder what I should put on the poster."

"Cute baby animals!" said Jack immediately. "Lambs, piglets and calves. We can't wait to see them all on Monday."

"And make it really colourful and bright,"

said Grace, looking at the faded poster on
the board, "so it really stands out."

A veterinary nurse came into the waiting
room. "Winston Turner, please," she
called.

"That's us," said the lady, getting up.
Winston heaved himself stiffly to his feet.
"Thanks for the advice on the poster! I'll
see you soon."

The twins said goodbye.

"That's a gorgeous puppy," said Carol
the receptionist, looking at Pip's picture
on the wall.

"Are you looking for a dog, Carol?"
Grace said hopefully.

"No, I've already got my two Cavalier
King Charles spaniels, and I don't think a
Border collie pup would lie quietly under

the desk here all day," said Carol. "But I'll keep my ears open for anyone who is looking for a puppy like that."

"Thanks!" the twins chorused.

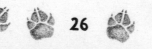

CHAPTER 4

"Have you got everything? Lunch box,
sun hats? Did you remember to use sun
cream?" asked Mum. Their teacher,
Ms Drew, was ticking off names on her
clipboard as their class boarded the coach
on Monday morning.

   27

"Yes, yes and yes," said Jack. "Hurry up, Grace, we don't want to make everyone wait for us."

"Coming," said Grace. She had Pip on a long lead as the little puppy yapped and tried to herd their class on to the bus.

"That's enough herding, Pip!" Grace

laughed. "Everyone's going where they should, don't worry. Are you going to put Pip in the puppy crate?" she asked her mother.

"No, I'll take him straight to Top Dog," said Mum. "He can come for a walk with the other dogs."

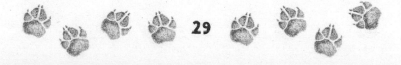

Grace and Jack stepped on to the coach.

"Be good, Pip," Jack called. "No running off to herd squirrels!"

Apple Tree Farm was a short coach ride away from school.

"Poo!" said Jack as he got off the coach. "What a stink."

"I think it smells nice," said Grace, breathing in the rich farmyard smell.

"Look, there's Winston!" said Jack as the old Labrador they had met at the vet's spotted them and ambled over to say hello. He sniffed at Grace and Jack's legs and wagged his tail.

"Wouldn't it be funny if humans greeted each other by sniffing to find out where they'd come from," giggled Grace.

A boy, slightly older than them, with

light-brown hair and freckles ran over.
"Hi, I'm Ben. Winston is my dog."

"We met him at the vet's the other day,"
Grace explained.

"And he can probably smell Pip, the
puppy we're looking after," said Jack. "I'm
Jack and this is Grace. We're twins."

"Winston and I are twins, too!" said Ben.
"We're both eleven and we have the exact
same birthday. I don't have any brothers
or sisters and Winston and I do everything
together. At least, we used to." Ben sighed.
"Winston always used to get up early to
help me with my farm jobs before school
but he doesn't do that so much since he
got arthritis." Ben stroked Winston's head.
"In dog years Winston's seventy-seven."

"That's ancient!" said Jack.

Ben nodded. "He's really happy today because it's a teacher-training day at my school and I can stay on the farm with him. Mum's asked if I can help out with your school trip – she's busy thinking of ways to advertise the farm."

Grace saw Ben's mum talking to one of their teachers. "When we met her at the vet's she said she wants to do some new posters."

Ben grinned. "We definitely need to. The posters we've got are almost as ancient as Winston!"

Ms Drew waved everyone from school over. Jack and Grace were put in a group with a parent helper. Ben and Winston tagged along with them as they went to the barn where the cows were kept.

    32

"Did you know that a cow has four
stomachs to digest their food with?" he
said as they entered the barn and saw a
line of cows munching on hay bales.

"That's a lot of stomachs," said Grace.
"Imagine having four tummies rumbling
when you're hungry!"

Ben laughed. "Cows do eat a lot. They're clever, too. They gather round the gate when it's time to be fed or milked. The chickens aren't so clever. They always think it's food time. Did you know that there are more chickens in the world than there are people?"

"Wow!" Jack was impressed. "You know loads about animals."

Ben beamed. "I love helping out on the farm and talking to visitors. The only job I don't like so much is looking after the really little kids. They're always running off then Mum makes me run after them. I could do with a sheepdog to help round them up!"

"A sheepdog!" gasped Grace, an idea spinning in her head. "Jack," she

   34

whispered, catching her brother's eye.

He nodded and she knew he was thinking the same. The farm would make a perfect home for Pip!

The words tumbled out of Grace. "Pip, the puppy we're looking after at the moment, is a Border collie. He's always trying to herd people and animals. Could you give him a forever home? He'd need to be trained, but you seem to know loads about animals, I bet you could do it."

"We'd have to ask you some questions first and do a home check," Jack added. "But I'm sure you'd pass them easily."

Grace brimmed with excitement. She could hardly believe it when Ben shook his head.

"Thanks, but Winston's too old to have a

puppy bothering him." Crouching down in front of Winston, Ben stroked his smooth black head and along his back. "And I love Winston too much to love another dog too."

Ben sounded very sure but Grace wasn't ready to give up. "You could at least think about it..." she began persuasively.

"Leave it, Grace," Jack whispered, seeing Ben shake his head. "Let's talk when we get home."

"All right," said Grace reluctantly. She crouched down beside Ben and Winston. "Well, if you change your mind just let us know." She fished a Forever Homes business card out of the pocket of her coat. "Here."

"Thanks," he said, pocketing the card. "But I won't change my mind. Winston's definitely the only dog for me!"

CHAPTER 5

After visiting the cows, Grace and Jack's
class went to the lambing barn and had a
wonderful time feeding the lambs bottles
of milk. After lunch they petted goats,
piglets and chickens, and at the end of
the day their team won a quiz about

farm animals.

"That was the best school trip ever!" shouted Grace as they burst in the front door. "Pip would love living on that farm."

They went to find the little puppy. He was in Top Dog's playroom nosing a ball around. He bounded over and plonked the ball at Grace's feet. Grace rolled it across the floor for him to chase. "It's so annoying that Ben doesn't want another dog," she said.

"I know," agreed Jack. "I bet he'd love having two dogs despite what he says. It's like having kids. There are four of us but Mum and Dad love us all the same."

"Well actually, they secretly love me best," said Grace, with a wicked grin.

"No, me!" Jack grinned. "But, seriously,

I'm sure Ben *could* love two dogs and I think Winston would like to have a puppy to play with."

"Hello, twins, how was the farm?" Mum asked, coming into the room.

"Brilliant. I held a baby chick," said Grace.

"I cuddled a piglet," said Jack. "It almost weed on me but luckily I'd just passed it on to Freddy."

"Not so lucky for Freddy," said their mother.

Jack chuckled. "Suppose not. Mum ... do older dogs usually cope OK if their owner gets a puppy?"

"It depends," said Mum. "Why?"

Between them, Grace and Jack explained about Ben and Winston.

Mum listened carefully. "I'm sure having Pip wouldn't make Ben love Winston any less and Pip might also be very good for Winston. Studies have shown that a puppy can give an older dog a new lease of life."

Grace was pleased. "So Ben could give Pip his perfect Forever Home. We've just got to convince him!"

"It does depend on the dogs," Mum warned. "Some older dogs can feel threatened if a younger dog comes along. You'd need to introduce them carefully and see how they got on."

"Why don't we take Pip to visit Ben and Winston at the farm?" said Grace. Then her face fell. "Oh, I just remembered. Dogs aren't allowed to visit the farm."

Jack thought for a moment. "What if we

ring Ben's mum and ask if she would let us bring Pip to see the animals? We could say that we want him to get used to them because we're hoping to find him a home on a farm."

"That's brilliant!" Grace exclaimed. "But we'd need a grown-up to take us there." She turned a winning smile on Mum.

Mum chuckled. "Are you quite sure the farm is the right home for Pip – and Ben the right owner?"

"Yes," said Grace and Jack together.

"All right, if Ben's mum agrees to the visit then I'll take you." Grace and Jack leapt on her for a group hug. "That's if I've got any breath left!" gasped Mum.

CHAPTER 6

First thing on Saturday morning, Grace and Jack loaded Pip into a crate in the back of their mum's van.

"Have you got the lead?" Jack said. "Ben's mum said Pip must be on a lead at all times."

"Quite right, too." Mum started up the engine. "An untrained dog can cause a lot of harm running loose among farm animals."

"Lead and harness, tick," said Grace, waggling them both at Jack.

"Let's go before the farm opens up to everyone else."

Half an hour later, they arrived in the car park at Apple Tree Farm.

Jack looked round. "Where's Ben? He was supposed to be meeting us here."

"Maybe he's busy with the animals," said Mum. "Leave Pip with me and see if you can find him."

"Let's try the barn first," said Grace

as they walked towards the deserted farmyard. "Ben might be feeding the piglets."

Ben wasn't in the barn though. Nor was

he in the milking parlour. Suddenly Jack spotted him by the farmhouse. He was kneeling and talking to something beside him.

Grace and Jack ran over and saw that Ben was talking to Winston, who was sitting next to a bowl full of food.

Ben looked up, and Grace saw that he looked sad. "What's the matter?" she asked.

"Winston won't touch his food this morning. He normally wolfs it down. Come on, boy," Ben encouraged the dog. "Try some breakfast."

The Labrador looked at him and gave a friendly huff but didn't take a bite. Ben sighed sadly. "Maybe it's because he's getting old," he said.

There was a small silence, then Grace broke it. "We've ... um ... brought Pip to look round the farm. Our mum's looking after him in the car park but we can go home if it's not a good time."

Ben swiped a hand across his face. "No, it's fine. Let's go and get your puppy and see what he makes of the animals."

Pip greeted Grace and Jack as if they'd been gone for years, his whole body wriggling as his tail wagged wildly from side to side.

He yapped loudly.

"Hello, you must be Ben," said Mum, raising her voice to be heard over Pip's excited barks. "I'm Sarah. Thanks for letting Pip visit your farm."

"Pip, you silly thing," said Grace giggling as she took him from her mother. "Your tail's wagging so hard it's making your bum wiggle."

"He's pretty cute," said Ben, managing a small smile as Pip greeted him with the same enthusiasm. He bent down to ruffle Pip's neck, his smile widening as Pip licked his nose then his hands. "You're a friendly pup, aren't you?"

"Pip loves people," said Jack.

"And animals," put in Grace.

Pip rolled over on his back, showing his pink tummy. Ben tickled him. "Do you like

that?" Ben said softly as Pip wriggled in delight. "Yes, you do, don't you? Winston was like you when he was a puppy..." Ben suddenly broke off and stood up, clearing his throat. "Right, we'd better get started. My mum said she'd love to meet you," he added to Mrs Taylor.

"That's very kind. I'd like to meet her, too," said Mum.

   49

Ben led them back to the farmhouse, ushering everyone in through the kitchen where his mum was rolling out cookie dough. "Hello, Mrs Turner," the twins called as they trooped in.

"Hello, everyone. Is this Pip? Well, aren't you gorgeous?" Wiping her doughy hands on her apron, Mrs Turner bent down to say hello. She laughed as Pip wriggled

    50

around. "So you're trying to find this little chap a home?"

"Yes, on a farm!" said Grace eagerly.

"His mum and dad were both working sheepdogs," said Jack. "And he's got way too much energy to be a house dog."

"He looks just like my first dog – Zak. He was a working collie too. He was the cleverest dog I've ever known – collies are more intelligent than us humans, sometimes!" Ben's mum laughed as Pip jumped around her legs. "You know, maybe we could have this little one here. We could do with a young dog around the place."

Grace's heart leapt. "That would be wonderful!"

But Ben was shaking his head. "We

don't need another dog, Mum. We've got Winston and he wouldn't like it."

His mum sighed. "OK, I won't get another dog if you don't want one, Ben. Why don't you kids take Pip round the farm. Have a seat, Sarah. I'll pop the kettle on."

Ben nodded. "Winston can come with us." He glanced around. "Where is he?" he said, his eyes falling on the empty dog bed.

"I thought he was with you," said Mrs Turner in surprise.

"He was but he seemed tired and wouldn't eat so I thought he had gone back to his bed," said Ben, frowning.

"He'll be out on the farm somewhere," said his mum reassuringly. "You know what he's like. He loves wandering round.

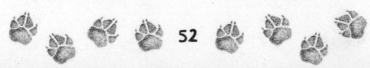

I think he feels it's his job to keep an eye on things," she explained to the twins. "I'm sure you'll find him while you're out with Pip. Go on, off you go!"

Pip yapped with excitement, straining against his harness as Grace and Jack followed Ben outside.

"Let's start with the sheep field," said Ben.

They headed out of the farmyard and along a path between the fields where the sheep and lambs lived. Pip kept straining on his lead, pulling Jack towards a copse of trees at the far end of the path.

"No, Pip, we're going this way," said Jack. "We're going to see the sheep in this field over here."

Pip whined and pulled towards the

trees again.

"Heel, Pip," said Jack firmly.

Reluctantly, Pip gave in and walked alongside the children but he kept twisting his head to look behind him. However, as they reached the gate, he caught sight of the sheep and was immediately distracted, pushing his nose against the fence and yapping excitedly.

The sheep nearest to the fence baaed in alarm and trotted away with her lamb at her heels.

"Now now, stop that," Ben said to Pip.
"Sheepdogs mustn't bark at sheep." He
rummaged in his pocket and pulled out a
treat. "Lie down," he said.

Pip flopped down. "Good boy," said Ben,
crouching down and giving him a treat.
"You be quiet and just watch," he said,
stroking Pip's back. Pip stayed lying down,
watching the sheep with his eager bright

eyes. A lamb wandered close to the fence.
Pip started to jump up, but Ben corrected
him instantly with his voice. "No, Pip!

    55

Down!" he said firmly. Pip glanced at him and then settled down again, his nose on his paws.

"There's a good pup," Ben said, fussing him and giving him another treat. Pip licked his hand.

Grace and Jack's eyes met. Ben obviously knew exactly how to handle a working dog. He would be the perfect owner and Apple Tree Farm would be the perfect home. But how could they persuade him?

"Pip's one of the easiest puppies we've ever had in," said Jack. "He's really clever."

"He's going to be a brilliant companion for someone," said Grace.

Ben looked at Pip for a moment and then his lips tightened. "You know, it's strange we haven't found Winston yet," he said, getting up. "Let's keep going."

They continued round the farm but they didn't find Winston anywhere. By the time they got back to the farmhouse, a deep frown was creasing Ben's forehead.

"Where is Winston?" he said. "We've been round the whole farm."

Grace was feeling very anxious too. She'd been sure they'd find the Labrador

somewhere.

"We must have missed him. Why don't we go out and look again?" she said.

"Yeah, he's got to be somewhere nearby," said Jack. "We'll help you find him, Ben."

Ben gave them a grateful look. "Thanks!"

They set off again, calling Winston's name.

CHAPTER 7

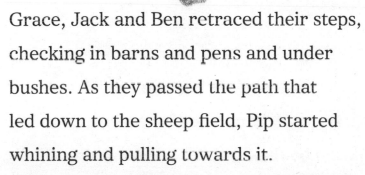

Grace, Jack and Ben retraced their steps,
checking in barns and pens and under
bushes. As they passed the path that
led down to the sheep field, Pip started
whining and pulling towards it.

"No, Pip!" said Jack. "Not that way."

"Here, I'll take him," offered Grace as they continued on towards the cow fields. But as they swapped over, Pip leapt forward and the lead slipped through their fingers. The twins both tried to grab it but Pip was too fast. He took off, ducking under the barbed wire fence and racing across the field of young cows.

"Pip, come back!" Jack yelled as the cows scattered in alarm.

Grace's heart banged painfully. "Pip!" she shouted, convinced he was going to be injured by the herd.

"He's heading towards the sheep field,"

said Ben. 'If we're quick we can cut him

off." He started running back to the path

with Grace and Jack chasing behind.

Grace ran as fast as she could, her arms

pumping. What if Pip got in with the sheep

and chased them? It could really scare

them.

"There he is!" Ben shouted.

Pip ran out of the cow field and

flashed across the path ahead of them.

Grace thought he was going to duck under

the gate into the sheep field but instead, he

veered left.

"Where's he going?" panted Jack.

"He's heading for those trees!" said Ben.

They all sprinted after the puppy, their breath coming in ragged gasps. As they reached the copse, Ben skidded to a halt. "Look!" he said, pointing. There was a hole in the fence's wire netting. A few clumps of white fluff were caught on the edges. Near to the hole, a worried-looking sheep was standing with a lamb at her side. "I have to fix that hole in case a lamb

escapes. But let's get Pip first," panted
Ben.

They ran into the trees. There was no
sign of the puppy at all. Grace looked
anxiously at Jack. *What if they didn't find
him?*

"Pip!" she shouted. "Pip, come!"

"*Yap! Yap! Yap!*"

"Over there!" said Jack. He and Ben
pushed through the trees and brambles.

Grace followed them, not caring about
the thorns that caught on her bare arms.
The next moment, she saw Pip pushing
through the undergrowth, coming to meet
them. "There you are!" she said, throwing
herself down on the ground to hug the
excited puppy. He licked her cheek but
before she could scoop him up, he turned

 63

and ran back through the bushes.

"No, Pip! Come back!" said Jack. But the puppy carried on, looking round at them every few steps.

"Wait," said Ben suddenly. "I think he wants us to follow him! What are you trying to show us, pup?" He pushed through the bushes until they reached a small clearing. "Oh!" he gasped. A lamb was caught in a patch of brambles, the thorns tangled in her fluffy coat. Winston was lying beside her, keeping her calm. Seeing the children, he thumped his tail.

"Winston!" cried Ben in relief. Pip bounced over to the older dog and jumped around him, licking at his mouth. Winston gently pushed him away with his nose and heaved himself up. Ben rushed over and

hugged him. "Oh, Winston, you must have
realised that a lamb had got out and come
to find it. Were you then too tired to come
and get me? Is that it? Thank goodness
Pip found *you*!" Pip pushed his little nose
under Ben's arms and Ben gathered him

   65

up in the hug. "What a good puppy you are," he said. "A great puppy. The best puppy. You found Winston and the lamb, didn't you?"

Pip wagged his tail proudly.

"He must have realised they needed help," Ben said, looking round at Grace and Jack. "Mum was right, Border collies are the cleverest dogs." He untangled the lamb. "Come on, let's take you back to the field, little one," he said, picking her up. "Your mum will be very worried about you."

Grace picked up Pip and she and Jack followed Ben out of the trees, with Winston at their heels. Pip licked Grace's chin and wagged his tail as she covered his head with kisses. She was sure he knew

   66

just how clever he had been!

When they reached the field, Ben climbed over the fence and put the lamb down with its mum and twin sister. The mum baaed happily, as both lambs dived underneath her and started to drink her milk, their little white tails waggling.

"Safe and sound," said Ben in satisfaction as he climbed back over the

fence. He took some string and a penknife from his pocket and tied the hole closed. "That'll do until I tell Dad and he can fix it properly. Clever dogs," he said, stroking Winston's head and then Pip's.

An idea suddenly came into Grace's head as she looked at the mother sheep. "Do you think that mother sheep wishes she only had one lamb?" she asked Ben suddenly.

He looked surprised. "Of course not."

"She loves both her lambs just the same, doesn't she?" Grace persisted.

"Yes," said Ben.

"Just like our mum loves both me and Jack equally," said Grace, fixing him with a look.

Ben stared at the sheep and her lambs

and then his eyes moved to Winston who was lying on the grass and Pip who was still in Grace's arms. "Are you trying to say that I could love a new puppy and still love Winston just the same?" he said slowly.

Grace and Jack both nodded hard.

Ben bit his lip. "But what about Winston? He might not like having another dog around."

"Why don't we see?" Jack said.

Grace put Pip down. He bounced over to Winston and yapped, sticking his bottom in the air as he invited the older dog to play.

"It's no good. Winston won't want to play –" Ben broke off in astonishment as Winston gave a deep woof and bounced back at Pip.

Pip leapt around in delight.

"Wow!" exclaimed Ben in disbelief as the dogs frolicked together. "That's the fastest I've seen Winston move in ages!"

"Mum says studies have shown that a puppy can give an older dog a new lease of life," said Jack.

Winston flopped down and rolled over, letting Pip pull at the thick fur around his neck. Both dogs play-growled and wagged their tails.

"So do you still think Winston wouldn't like having Pip around?" said Grace, glancing at Ben.

The corners of his mouth twitched and then a wide smile spread across his face. "No. OK. You're right. You've convinced

me!" Kneeling down, Ben stroked both
dogs. "So, Pip, would you like to live here
and be a farm dog?"

Pip yapped.

Jack grinned. "I think that's a yes from
Pip!" he said.

CHAPTER 8

Mrs Taylor was delighted when she heard the news. "It'll be lovely to have a Border collie. Maybe you can even enter some sheepdog trials when he's ready."

"That would be awesome," said Ben. He picked up Pip. "I bet you'd like that,

wouldn't you, boy? He's so clever, Mum.
You should have seen the way he led us to
Winston and the lamb!"

Grace and Jack swapped looks. It was
wonderful to hear Ben enthusing about
Pip. Grace sidled up to Jack. "We don't
need to do an official home check this
time, do we?"

Jack shook his head. "No, I think we've
seen all we need. This is definitely the
perfect home for Pip. We'll have to tell
Jess and Alex."

"And when they've had their baby, they'll
be able to bring it to the farm for a visit!"
Happiness rushed through Grace as she
looked at Ben cuddling the little puppy. Pip
was actually starting to look tired for once.
She heaved a delighted sigh. Everything

had worked out wonderfully after all!

A few weeks later, Grace and Jack returned to Apple Tree Farm to see how Pip was getting on. They found Ben in the yard, helping show a party of preschool children around. The children were gathered round a pen of pygmy goats. Pip and Winston sat either side of him, their eyes on Ben, waiting for him to say that they could move.

"Wow! Look at that!" Jack exclaimed as he approached. Pip had clearly recognised the twins. His body quivered with excitement and his tail swished from side to side but he remained where he was.

"He's being so good!" said Grace as
Ben gave him the command to go free
and he bounded over. "And hasn't he
grown? Hello, boy," she said as Pip rushed
between her and Jack, licking their hands
before darting back to Ben.

Winston ambled over, his tail wagging.

Ben's eyes shone. "Pip's great. He and Winston get on really well and Pip's a brilliant farm dog. Pip definitely keeps Winston young, and I think Winston is teaching Pip to be a bit calmer!"

Just then, a woman's voice rang out from the crowd of children. "Oliver, come back!" A small boy, bored of the goats, had wandered away from the group.

"Pip." Ben nodded at the little boy. "On."

Pip's ears pricked. Immediately, he peeled away from Ben and trotted after the child.

"Come by," called Ben softly. The puppy swung left, going clockwise in a circle around the toddler, gently herding him by nudging him with his nose.

The little boy started giggling as he

toddled back to the group.

"I want a go," called a little girl who was watching. "Please, can the doggy catch me?"

Ben called Pip over and patted him. "Good boy!" He pulled a ball from his pocket and gave it to Pip. "Reward time. Go and play."

Pip took the ball and brought it to the little girl. He dropped it at her feet.

"That'll keep him busy for a while," said Ben with a grin. "All the kids will want a turn and Pip never gets tired of fetching it for them."

Grace couldn't stop smiling. "I'm so happy it's all worked out."

"It really has," said Ben. "And have you seen the new posters Mum's made?"

The twins shook their heads. Ben led them over to the play barn where there was a new poster in the window. At the top in big bright letters were the words: "Apple Tree Farm". Beneath, there was a picture of Pip and Winston, looking incredibly cute as they sat together with their ears pricked and tongues hanging out. At the bottom it said: "Come and meet us and our friends here at Apple Tree Farm."

"We've had lots of people visiting since Mum put them up," said Ben. He looked proudly at Pip and Winston. "They're the perfect poster dogs – and the perfect dogs for me!" He smiled at the twins. "Thanks for not giving up when I said I didn't want Pip."

"We don't give up easily," said Grace, swapping smiles with Jack.

Ben grinned. "Yeah, I worked that out!"

The twins gave Pip a last cuddle and went to find their mum.

"I love a happy ending," said Grace.

"Me too," said Jack. "It was such a good idea to point out to Ben that the mother sheep loved both her lambs equally."

"Thanks." Grace shot him a sideways look. "Though you know, what I said about

Mum wasn't exactly true."

Jack frowned. "What do you mean?"

Grace's eyes twinkled with mischief.

    81

"Well, *obviously* Mum loves me more. I mean, I know she pretends to love us both the same but I'm definitely her favourite..."

"No way, I'm her favourite!" said Jack.

"Uh – no, I am!" said Grace.

She squealed and dodged as Jack threw a handful of hay at her. He chased after her and, laughing and arguing, they raced through the farm to the car.

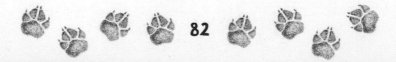

MRS TAYLOR'S FACT FILE

NAME: Sarah Anne Taylor

AGE: Forty-four

LIKES: Dogs, cats, spending time with family and friends, going for long walks in the countryside

DISLIKES: People who are cruel to animals, mess and rudeness

FAVOURITE COLOUR: Aquamarine

HOBBIES: Pilates, reading and walking

FAVOURITE FOODS: Home-made lasagne, salted caramel chocolate

FAVOURITE JOKE:

Q: What do you call a snowman's dog?

A: A slush puppy!

DREAM JOB: Running Top Dog!

WHAT ANIMAL WOULD YOU BE? A snow leopard roaming the Himalayan mountains.

DASTARDLY DOGGY WORD SCRAMBLE

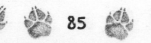

Unscramble the letters to find the hidden doggy word. If you get all six right take a big bow (wow!).

1. deal   **2.** llaroc

3. ypupp

4. istelwh   **5.** cliloe

6. heeps dgo rilats

ANSWERS ON PAGE 90

GRACE AND JACK'S FAVOURITE DOG JOKES!

WHAT DID THE HUNGRY DALMATIAN SAY WHEN HE HAD SOME DOG FOOD?

That hits the spot!

WHAT KIND OF DOG DID DRACULA HAVE?

A bloodhound!

WHAT'S A DOG'S FAVOURITE MUSICAL INSTRUMENT?

A trom-bone!

**WHAT DO YOU GET WHEN YOU CROSS
A SHEEPDOG WITH A ROSE?**

A collie-flower!

Are you a **TOP DOG**?

Can you answer **Grace** and **Jack's** questions on the jobs dogs were bred to do?

1. **WHICH OF THE FOLLOWING ARE OFTEN USED AS POLICE DOGS:**

    a) German Shepherd

    b) Husky

    c) Labrador

    d) Border Collie

2. **WHICH OF THE FOLLOWING ARE OFTEN USED AS DOGS TO HERD SHEEP:**

    a) German Shepherd

    b) Husky

c) Labrador

d) Border Collie

3. **WHICH OF THE FOLLOWING ARE MOST COMMONLY USED AS GUIDE DOGS:**

    a) German Shepherd

    b) Husky

    c) Labrador

    d) Border Collie

4. **WHICH OF THE FOLLOWING WERE TRADITIONALLY BRED TO PULL SLEDS:**

    a) German Shepherd

    b) Husky

    c) Labrador

    d) Border Collie

ANSWERS ON PAGE 90

ANSWERS TO QUIZ ON PAGE 85

1. lead **2.** collar **3.** puppy **4.** whistle

5. collie **6.** sheep dog trials

ANSWERS TO QUIZ ON PAGE 88-89

1)a 2)d 3)c 4)b